¾ **cup** of milk (buttermilk works bes

1 **teaspoon** of pure vanilla extract

Once you have measured the milk and vanilla into a measuring cup, put to the side.

Next, mix the sifted dry ingredients into the large bowl of butter, sugar, and eggs. Next, scoop the dry mixture into the batter in three steps: Stir the batter after each addition, adding some of the milk after each step. Mix until smooth, but don't overbeat or the cupcakes will be tough instead of tender.

Finally, spoon the mixed batter into the individual cups, 2/3 full or the cupcakes will overflow when baking and make a big mess.

Once the batter is in the pans, have your adult helper place the pans in the middle rack of the oven and set the timer for 22 minutes.

Wait and watch. Once they are baked, ask your helper to remove the pans to cool on a rack.

When the cupcakes are completely cool, they are ready for frosting.

A frosting recipe is at the back of this book.

Caution: It is imperative that young children have an adult assist them when making the recipe in this book—especially when using electrical appliances and all ovens

Baby Cakes

by **Theo Heras**
Illustrations by **Renné Benoit**

paj̈amapress

Time to bake!

Put on an apron.

Here are a big bowl
and measuring cups
and spoons.

Need lots
of ingredients.

Kitty wants
to help.

Measure flour.

Put it in the bowl.
Oops!

No, Kitty!

Sprinkle salt,
but not too much.

Don't forget the
baking powder.

Creaming the butter
is hard work.

Sugar on fingers
sure is sweet.

Wash hands.

Uh oh!
Eggs are
easy to
break!

Kitty laps them up.

Wash hands.

Try again.

Pour milk.

Blend vanilla.

Mix and mix and mix.

Kitty wants to mix too.

Fill cups.

Mommy puts them in the oven to bake.

Wait and wait and wait.

Out come Baby Cakes.

Time for tea!

First published in the United States and Canada in 2017

www.pajamapress.ca   info@pajamapress.ca

  Canada Council Conseil des arts    ONTARIO ARTS COUNCIL   Canadä
for the Arts   du Canada   CONSEIL DES ARTS DE L'ONTARIO
                                                 an Ontario government agency
                                                 un organisme du gouvernement de l'Ontario

The publisher gratefully acknowledges the support of the Canada Council for the Arts and the Ontario Arts Council for its publishing program. We acknowledge the financial support of the Government of Canada through the Canada Book Fund (CBF) for our publishing activities.

Library and Archives Canada Cataloguing in Publication

Heras, Theo, author
Baby cakes / by Theo Heras ; illustrations by Renné Benoit.
ISBN 978-1-77278-030-7 (hardcover)
I. Benoit, Renné, illustrator II. Title.
PS8615.E687B33 2017   jC813'.6   C2017-900686-X

Publisher Cataloging-in-Publication Data (U.S.)

Names: Heras, Theo, 1948-, author. | Benoit, Renné, illustrator.
Title: Baby Cakes / by Theo Heras ; illustrations by Renné Benoit.
Description: Toronto, Ontario Canada : Pajama Press, 2017. | Summary: "Baby and his older sister are helping with the baking, but kitty wants to help too. After some mischief, messes, and minor mishaps, everybody gets to enjoy the treats together"
— Provided by publisher. Identifiers: ISBN 978-1-77278-030-7 (hardcover)
Subjects: LCSH: Cooking – Juvenile fiction. | Clothing and dress -- Juvenile fiction.
| Brothers and sisters – Juvenile fiction. | Kittens – Juvenile fiction. | BISAC: JUVENILE FICTION / Cooking & Food.
| JUVENILE FICTION / Family / Siblings. | JUVENILE FICTION / Humorous Stories.
Classification: LCC PZ7.H473Bab |DDC [E] – dc23

Designed by Rebecca Bender

Manufactured by Qualibre Inc./Print Plus
Printed in China

Pajama Press Inc.
181 Carlaw Ave. Suite 207 Toronto, Ontario Canada, M4M 2S1

Distributed in Canada by UTP Distribution
5201 Dufferin Street Toronto, Ontario Canada, M3H 5T8

Distributed in the U.S. by Ingram Publisher Services
1 Ingram Blvd. La Vergne, TN 37086, USA

**Original art
created in watercolor
and digital**

Vanilla Frosting

1  stick of butter, softened (1/2 cup)

3  **cups** of icing sugar

¼ **teaspoon** of salt

2 **tablespoons** of cream

1 **teaspoon** of pure vanilla extract

In a large mixing bowl, cream the butter with a wooden spoon until it is very smooth.*

Set the sifter inside a medium mixing bowl and add icing sugar and salt.

Gradually sift the icing sugar and salt in small amounts into the bowl of smooth butter, continually beating the mixture until smooth.

Keep adding the remaining icing sugar and beat until it feels a little firm, then add the cream and vanilla. Continue to beat until the cream and vanilla are mixed in and the icing is fluffy.

*This icing recipe is much easier to make with the help of an electric hand mixer. If one is available, ask your adult helper to assist you with using this piece of equipment.